NOT HUMAN

Wesley Hall, Jr.

www.TrueVinePublishing.org

Not Human
Wesley Hall, Jr.

Published by True Vine Publishing Co.
810 Dominican Dr. Ste. 103
Nashville, TN 37228
www.TrueVinePublishing.org

ISBN: 978-1-956469-53-0 Paperback
ISBN: 978-1-956469-54-7 eBook

Printed in the United State of America—First Printing

DEDICATION

To Francine, DeAnthony, and The Geek Shack Crew, thank you for all your help and support on this new journey.

TABLE OF CONTENTS

TABLE OF CONTENTS

WELCOME TO THE FAMILY

It was our third date, and I knew I had to tell her about my family. As we lay down on a grassy hilltop with my back on the ground, Amy's head rested on my chest. I had pondered the possibility of what I was going to tell her about how my family is. The thing about my family was the fact that my mother had just served a long time in the Defense Attorney's Office as a lawyer, while my father on the other hand, his job had gained him a good opportunity to travel overseas and he's doing business somewhere over in Germany. I don't get to see him a lot and he rarely calls so I don't think I necessarily have to tell him about Amy, right?

These thoughts filled my mind as I stared up at the clear blue sky. I felt a tug on my t-shirt as I glanced down to see Amy.

"Hey, you okay?" she asked me as I tried to sit up. Amy eased up off my chest and landed on her back next to me.

"Yeah, I'm fine. I was just thinking about where would be a good place for us to go next on this adventure of ours." I told her as I pulled out my phone and started to scroll through different movie titles to find something that Amy would like. I had a feeling she would love it if I chose an action film or even a horror mystery film.

"Well is there anywhere you would like to go, Amy?" I asked her as I looked into her sea blue eyes. She lay there and tapped her chin as she pondered the question I had asked.

"Oh!" She exclaimed as she sat up fast and looked at me like she was on the verge of jumping up and down like a kid in a candy store. "I think we should go to an ice cream shop than a movie afterward!" Amy said joyfully as she sprang to her feet like a spring coil.

I was startled when Amy had gotten excited at first. When she gave me her response, I didn't know what to think— especially about the Ice cream shop, which threw me for a loop. So I put into my phone the nearest ice cream shop and the location I had received on my phone was not that far away from where we were.

"Okay, sure we can go to the ice cream shop before we head out to see a movie. Is there any movie in particular that you want to see?" I asked as I got to my feet and dusted off the grass that might have been left on my pants legs and shirt. I offered my hand to help Amy steady herself as she stood up.

"There was one film I wanted to see and I think it was called 'The Day the Last Flame Went Out,'" Amy told me as I had pulled out my phone yet again to see if I could find the movie that she was talking about. The weird thing was that for some reason the movie that Amy wanted to see was not showing up on my movie app.

"Huh?... That's weird? Hey, Amy, do you know what genre this movie is?" I asked her as I started to walk in the direction of the ice cream shop. Amy had made her way over to me at a steady jog.

"Um... Let me think. If memory serves correctly, I think the movie is a horror genre," Amy had questioned herself before telling me. As we continued to walk down the street toward the shop, I noticed my friend Marcus who was coming out of a video game store.

"Hey, Marcus!" I called out to him as he ran across the street to meet us.

"Hey man, what's up?" Marcus asked me as we gave each other a hug and a fist bump.

"Aw you know; nothing much. Just about to take my girlfriend Amy here to the ice cream shop then we are going to head to the movies right after," I told him.

He looked at me and gave a questionable nod then look at Amy and said, "Hey but, you wouldn't mind if I talked to my friend here for a little bit, do you?"

Amy looked at Marcus as if he was some random stranger who wanted to talk about something with me which must have had to be important. She gave him a sweet genuine smile and then said, "Sure you can talk with him, but can you do it when we get to the ice cream shop?"

Marcus crossed his arms while still holding on to the bag that he bought. Then he looked at a coffee shop next door to us and said, "you know, or we could go into here and get a snack while I talk to him."

Amy and I looked at the coffee shop and I said, "okay sure, Marcus we can talk for a little bit."

As the three of us walked into the shop, Amy said, "Hey I'm going to go and order us some drinks and maybe some cake. Could you two go ahead and grab us some seats."

"Sure, we can do that," I told her as she went and stood in a small line leading up to the cashier counter.

Marcus led me into the back of the coffee shop and then pushed me into the corner booth.

"Hey man, what's going on?" I said to him as I tried to adjust myself in the booth, so I didn't feel like I was being pinned to a wall. While Marcus had slid himself into the booth on the other side leaning on the table giving me an intense glare.

"Look, dude, you need to listen to me and listen well," Marcus said.

"Okay man, calm down. You're starting to scare me. What's going on?" I asked shakily.

"Don't you think something isn't right with this picture you're in right now?" Marcus asked.

"What are you talking about dude?" I asked.

Marcus sighed then said, "Okay, I'm going to ask you a very important question and I need you to answer it truthfully and honestly."

I looked around the corner of the booth to see how far Amy had gotten in the line. There were five people still in front of her ordering drinks. I turned back and looked at Marcus, nodded at him and said, "okay so I'll answer your question to the utmost truth that I can."

"Okay, here it goes. Where is Jackie?" Marcus asked with a determined look on his face to figure out if I knew the correct answer to his question.

I looked at Marcus and said "Look, man, I know we are friends and all but I have to ask you. Who is Jackie?"

Marcus's mouth fell open. The shocked look on his face was as if the whole world came crashing down around him.

"No, no, no, this can't be true. Hey come on man please tell me this is just some joke about how you don't know who Jackie is?" he said in a whisper so only I could hear what he was saying.

I shook my head.

"No Marcus. I'm telling you I have no clue who this Jackie person is. If you know who she is then please enlighten me?" I asked him trying to comprehend what was going on with my friend whom I had known since sophomore year of high school.

"How do you not remember Jackie?" Marcus said as he reached into his vest and pulled out a small wallet-sized photo of me with my dark chocolate skin wearing blue jeans and a black hoodie. The girl standing next to me with each of our arms wrapped around one another's shoulders had light mocha skin and curly black hair that was in a ponytail while wearing a blue hoodie and dark blue jeans.

"So I'm going to take it that the girl in this photo is Jackie?" I asked as I looked at him.

Marcus nodded then said "yep and to you, she is your best friend and not just that but she is your girlfriend. The two of you have been dating for three years now. I find it weird that you have been dating Jackie for so long and now I see you with some other girl and you two seem close. Not cool man."

Amy had placed her order and started waiting for her drinks to finish.

I took a snapshot of the photo of this Jackie and me from what looked to be like our first year in college.

"Hey Marcus, before you leave, can I ask you something?" I asked.

"Sure, what is it?" Marcus said as he inched his way out of the booth.

"Well, have you ever heard of a horror film called *The Day the Last Flame Went Out*?" I questioned.

Marcus gave me a questionable look and then said: "Dude I have never heard of that movie and I'm a huge movie geek, but nothing like that I don't think the movie exists."

Then Marcus left wishing me good luck with whatever I was going to encounter.

So in the end, Amy and I did not make it to the ice cream shop or the movies. Instead, she drove us straight to my house, and on the way there, she made a strange and dark declaration.

"I don't like annihilation but I know it's necessary," she said.

"Wait what did you just say?" I asked.

"Oh, nothing," she answered.

We arrived at the front door of my home and I told Amy "Hey my family is a little interesting, but whatever you see behind this door just try and dismiss it."

"I will try my best," Amy said.

I opened the door. The living room was set up like a courtroom. The place where the jury sits was one couch accompanied by three chairs set up right behind. For the Defendant and the Prosecutor, two black chairs sat on either side of a white table in the middle of the room. Where the Judge would sit in the front of the courtroom to oversee what was going on was represented by a dark brown recliner chair.

"Umm... what in the world is going on here?" I asked.

My mother was sitting in the recliner chair facing me wearing black pants and a long white button-down shirt. On my left in the section of the Jury sat my brother De, Jhai my sister, and the youngest sister Kami.

"Hey Wesley, Welcome back home, how are you doing?" Mom asked me.

"I'm good, Mom. How are you?" I replied.

Mom didn't answer me. She had her eyes fixed on Amy.

"Who might you be?" Mom asked.

"Oh, Mom this is my girlfriend" I started to say.

"No, Wesley!" Mom snapped at me.

I started to shake from the nerves in my body going out of whack from the sound of my mom's voice telling me no. My body had grown cold as if I was in a grave.

Mom looked back at Amy and said "So you are the one who did something to Jackie?"

Amy didn't respond.

I look at Amy in shock to see how silent she was.

"Well explain yourself. Is any of what she said true?" I asked her.

De and Jhai slowly made their way to the front door to block Amy's escape route.

"Girl explain yourself, now!" Mom demanded.

Amy was about to respond when there was a sudden knock at the door.

ABANDONED

Kim paced back and forth on the old rickety wooden floorboards of an abandoned apartment complex.

She thought back to how she ended up in this situation. Unknown to Kim, she had woken up a few minutes ahead of time while her head spun. She sat in a fancy dining chair while her hands had been bounded behind her by some rough and tight rope as it chafed against her skin.

"Huh? How long was I out?" Kim said as she tried to get her hands free from the rope binding.

As she sat in the chair wearing blue jeans, a white T-shirt, and a black leather trench coat that covered the t-shirt, Kim reached her tied hands into the outside pocket of the trench coat as she clasped her hands around a small hunting knife, in which the hilt was being held together by worn-down leather and duct tape. Kim turned the tool in her hands till the blade was up against the rope. She moved the blade steadily, but roughly to get her hands free. She looked around the room that she was sitting in and to Kim's surprise, the room was a disaster (like a tornado crashed through the walls and tore the place apart).

"Hello?" She said, listening for a response from anyone, but there was nothing.

The rope that kept her hands tied started to unravel after the knife cut through the rope like butter. Kim stood up and saw a large dark purple fabric couch that was ripped up as cotton puffed out of cushions and half of the couch that was cut leaned like a seesaw teetering on falling into the room below. There was a coffee table that had been smashed to bits as unreadable newspapers scattered across the floor.

"What in the world?" She said as she knelt to get a closer look at the newspaper that was down by her feet. As she picked up the paper, drops of blood dripped onto the old gray pages of the paper spelling out a word. The word RUN was sprawled across the paper in big red letters. Kim had dropped the newspaper to the floor as she made her way to the door with shaky hands. She reached for the doorknob and pulled on it. The door was locked, as it was being protected by two padlocks.

"Okay, I need to find a key." She said to herself, as she walked back into the living room and started lifting pieces of the coffee table that were smashed. To no avail the key was not there. Kim moved over to the couch and moved some of the cushions and there were some dimes and pennies, but no key. Kim made her way into the filthy kitchen that housed many different creatures from cockroaches to rats, but still no key.

"Where the hell is this key? I need to get out of here," she said frustrated, as she walked back into the living room and looked at the fireplace. The red brick base was falling apart. Above the fireplace was a picture of a large golden key that looked like it could open a treasure chest. Kim bent down and started dusting off the base of the fireplace to see if the key was there, and it wasn't.

"Come on, where in the world can this key be? I have checked everywhere." She said, as she stood up and searched the different bedrooms. The key was nowhere to be found. Then a moment of clarity hit Kim as she walked back into the living room.

"Oh wait?" she said, as she looked back at the picture of the key that hung over the fireplace.

"I didn't think to check behind the picture," Kim said, as she grabbed the picture and slowly leaned it up against the red brick of the fireplace. Hanging on a nail was a long black wire with two silver keys hanging off the end.

"Bingo. Now I can get out of this place." She said, as she snatched the keys from its hook and ran to the door to unlock the double padlocks. She inserted the first key into the lock and turned. The lock opened. Then Kim inserted the second key into the other padlock and turned the lock open. Kim swung open the door and down a long dark hallway, there was a door bathed in white light.

She ran with all her might to the exit, unaware of what awaited her on the other side. As Kim passed through the door. She found herself standing in a white padded room with a large reflective mirror facing her on the center wall. Kim looked at herself in the mirror to see that her clothes had changed to all white. She ran to a silver door with a small window. Kim clawed at the door, but there was no way to open it. She banged on the door screaming, "Let me out!"

BRUTAL BETRAYAL

Explosions could be heard as a war was going on out-side. Michael and Pearl stood in the hallway of an old Mansion that the owner had left behind when the war broke out. Soldiers could be heard entering the bottom floor of the mansion while they searched different rooms.

"Hey Pearl? Can you kind of hurry up and open that door," Michael said, as he walked down the hall and peeked around the corner to see if any soldiers had spotted them.

Pearl kneeled on one knee, took out a silver pin from her curly hair, and stuck it into the doorknob's lock.

"All right, all right. I got you. Just watch our backs," Pearl said, as she concentrated on picking the lock to get the door open.

"Hey, Michael? you do remember why we are here right," said Pearl.

Michael walked back over to Pearl as she was still working on the door to get it unlocked.

"Yeah, our mission is to get into this room and take the documents and get the hell out of here," Michael said.

The doorknob clicked as it was unlocked. "Nice. there we go," Pearl said, as she and Michael opened the door and slid themselves into the room. The room was lit by the afternoon sunlight as it beamed on the wooden office floor.

A large wooden desk sat in the middle of the room. Michael made his way over to the desk and found a black flash drive sitting on top of a large manila envelope.

"Pearl come over here and bring your bag. Hurry up so we can get the hell out of here," Michael said, as Pearl moved over to where he was behind the desk.

Pearl opened a midnight black backpack and slid the envelope inside as Michael put the flash drive into his blue jean pocket. Soldiers could be heard moving quickly up the stairs and through halls heading to their position.

"Come quick. We have to find a way out of here," Pearl said.

The office door kicked in as the house shook from the explosions going off outside. A man in a dark green jumpsuit with black leather boots strolled into the room.

"You two aren't going anywhere until you answer my questions," he said. He had a silver name tag that was pinned to the front of his jumpsuit. The name read Carnal.

"Oh snap," Michael whispered. Pearl zipped up her bag and slung it across her shoulder.

"What is it that you want? Carnal," Pearl said.

"I want the two of you to join my side. To help me win this war," Carnal said, as he stepped towards the desk.

"Sorry, bud. But that's not our problem," Michael said.

"Oh well? that's too bad," Carnal said.

When a tall bulky soldier came into the room wearing black survival gear like Michael and Pearl.

"Take the guy," Carnal said.

The bulky soldier rushed toward Michael tackling him to the ground wrapping his hands around Michael's throat and started to squeeze.

Michael started to throw punches at the soldier to break free, but every punch he threw felt like he was hitting a brick wall.

"Help...help," Michael said. As he struggled to breathe.

"Michael, No," Pearl said. As she tried to make her way over to him only to be stopped by Carnal.

"So, what will it be? are you going to join my side or let your partner die?" Carnal said.

What should I do? I already have the documents. She glanced at the door, *I should just run. But I can't just leave Michael here to die*, Pearl thought.

Pearl pushed Carnal out the way as she ran and drop-kicked the bulky soldier off Michael. Michael staggered to his feet and tried to catch his breath. They both moved towards the window.

"If you want us, then come and get us," Pearl said. As she and Michael jumped out the window falling into the forest below.

Once they landed on the earthy soil, Michael brushed himself off and searched himself to make sure he still had the flash drive from the mansion.

"Hey, do you still have the Flash Drive?" Pearl said as she turned around to look at him

Michael patted himself down and reached into his pocket to feel the flash drive with his fingertips.

"I have it," Michael said.

Pearl secured her bag on her back and started walking farther into the woods.

"Cool! We need to get moving. Carnal and his men are probably out looking for us," Pearl said.

Michael followed close behind Pearl as he thought back on how they got their hands on the information for the documents to steal. The way Michael received the info on what the documents looked like was not from a phone call but through a text message with only a few words that read.

"Look for the black drive. Don't let it fall into the wrong hands; and, for a partner bring someone you can trust."

As Michael walked, he looked at Pearl and thought.

I wonder if Pearl and Carnal know each other?

"Hey Pearl? Can I ask you something," Michael said.

"Sure. What's on your mind?" Pearl asked.

"Well? Do you and Carnal know one another?"

Pearl thought back to a day when she was sitting on a black metal bench in a garden with different arrangement of flowers from red roses to sunflowers and even a rare spider lily. The flowers lead up to a cliff side. The wind passed Pearl as she watched the sun going down. A man walked by and sat down next to her.

"I knew you would be here." The man said. He wore a black blazer, blue jeans and gray sneakers.

"Oh hey, Carnal, what's up." Pearl said.

"Do I need to go over the plan once more?" Carnal asked.

Pearl sat up and looked at Carnal.

"What's the point? I mean, what do you have that might give us an upper hand?" Pearl said.

Carnal looked at Pearl.

"The idea I came up with will give us an edge in this fight for a change." Carnal said.

Carnal took Pearl's hand and said "Once this war is over, only then can we finally go on that island trip you wanted to go on."

Pearl blushed at the thought.

Pearl hesitated before answering.

"No, I don't know him. Why do you ask Michael?"

Soldiers could be heard searching for them off in the distance of the woods.

"It's because you know when Carnal and his men showed up. You seemed more annoyed than anything when he barged his way into the office."

"Look. Just drop the whole idea of thinking that I and Carnal know one another."

Leaves on the ground crunched under footsteps and tree branches snapped like pencils as something moved in Michael and Pearl's direction.

Michael hid behind a tree and stood still like a statue to make himself unnoticeable to the enemy, whom he assumed was approaching. Pearl ducked behind some bushes and looked through them to see silhouettes of people. The first silhouette seemed to be tall with a muscular build. The second silhouette seemed to be that of a female. Her build was medium and slender reaching up to the first silhouette's shoulder.

As the two humanoid silhouettes came closer into view, both of them were wearing black hooded vests that were zipped, ripped jeans from hiking through the forest, and chocolate brown hiking boots.

"I'm telling you, Sam? This is just crazy, why would we meet them if they weren't going to be in the meeting spot, to begin with?" said the tall guy.

His partner put her hands to her lips, then looked at him.

"Will you please keep your voice down Robbi? If you have not noticed, we are in enemy territory," Sam said.

"You're right sorry. We need to stay on guard," Robbi said.

Michael and Pearl looked at each other from their hiding spots and formulated a plan. Pearl motioned to Michael that he was going to tackle the guy to get the jump on him while she went and took care of the girl.

"Robbi, make sure to be aware of your surroundings. Something doesn't feel right," Sam said.

"Yeah, I know what you mean. It feels like we are being watched," Robbi said, as he turned his back to the tree line.

Michael and Pearl rushed Robbi and Sam simultaneously knocking them both to the ground and placing

Robbi's and Sam's arms behind their backs to restrain them.

"Who are you two? Are you with Carnal and his men?" Michael said.

Sam had turned her head to see one of the captors kneeling next to Robbi holding his arms and not letting Robbi squirm around to try and escape.

"What? No, we are not with Carnal. Who the heck is Carnal? Release us and then we'll talk," Sam said.

Robbi tried to wiggle out of the tight grip that Michael had him in,

"Yeah! For all, we know you could be working on the same side as us."

Pearl heard a radio go off then looked at Michael as if to say, "Any more time here and those soldiers will be on us."

Michael and Pearl got to their feet and hoisted Sam and Robbi to their feet.

"Okay look. We need to get going," Michael said.

The two of them released Sam and Robbi. Sam looked at Michael to see if he was the person she and Robbi were supposed to meet.

"Hey? what's your name special ops dude?" Sam said.

"My name is Michael. I take it you're Sam," Michael said.

Robbi looked at Pearl and started to back away from her.

"You! Michael, I'm getting a strange aura from your partner," Robbi said.

The Soldiers were closing in on the group's location.

"Look, if we are done with introductions. We need to move," Pearl said.

The group ran ever deeper into the woods until they stumbled upon an old shack.

"I think we can hide in there for a while. Till the soldiers pass by," Robbi said.

Michael and Sam entered the shack first and upon them stepping on the wooden floor it gave under their weight and collapsed revealing a large cemented floor below. Sam and Michael picked themselves up off the cold ground and saw a narrow pathway in front of them.

"Hey, Michael? Can I ask you something?" Sam asked.

"Sure what's up?" Michael said.

Sam pulled a picture from her vest pocket and showed it to him. She shined a flashlight at the photo so Michael could see it. The photo was of him and a girl with long blond hair under the photo were two names, Michael and Angel.

"You were given this mission right? You came to this country with a partner who was a longtime friend," Sam said.

"Yeah, and the partner I came with was Pearl. Wasn't it?" Michael said.

"No, it wasn't. The person you came with was named Angel." Sam said.

"What? No, you're lying. No way that happened." Michael said.

Sam leaned in close to Michael.

"That girl Pearl. She might be working for the enemy. Carnal," Sam said.

Robbi and Pearl made their way down to their companions and saw the narrow pathway.

"I think Robbi and Sam should go. Then Michael and I will follow after," Pearl said.

Pearl picked up a small wooden floorboard and hid it behind her back as she watched Sam and Robbi make their way through the pathway.

"Hey, I think I see light. We can probably get out this way," Sam said.

Pearl stepped toward Michael.

"Hey? Michael." Pearl said.

"What is it, Pearl," Michael said.

"I don't know how to tell you this. But …" Pearl said.

Michael froze in place afraid of what Pearl was going to say.

"I've been working with Carnal. I'm Sorry," Pearl said.

With tears in her eyes as she swung the floorboard cracking Michael in the back of the head and knocking him out. Pearl searched through Michael's pockets and found the flash drive she needed to deliver to Carnal.

TOO HEAVY A BURDEN TO CARRY ALONE

A mountain of papers hung over Robbi's desk as he was deep into his work. His fingers danced across his keyboard as if on fire. Sweat dripped down his face as he frantically wrote out a report detailing the sitting of a mythical creature that had been seen a couple of months ago. The weight of multiple projects that Robbi wanted to get done was bearing down on him like a ball and chain drowning him in an ocean of work due to all the scattered spiral notebooks sprawled out around his office. On his oak desk sat a picture of two people, the first figure was of a woman with long brown hair that was tied in a ponytail. She had hazel brown eyes and wore a light gray hoodie that read: "We protect each other." The girl's arm was wrapped around another person, a boy, who had curly black hair, one white eye, and the other was brown. He wore the same hoodie as the girl, only his read: "At Least we try to." The pair wore blue jeans and they had bright smiles on their faces.

Robbi leaned back in his chair and looked up at the ceiling staring at what felt like a black void. He let out a sigh, "Why does this always happen to me?" he said.

That picture on his desk of him and his friend Valery brought back so many memories. I think that photo was taken at a convention called Black Ash Birds. This was when the two of them were in their Sophomore year of college. On that day something like me a shadow became aware of my existence. Most times I tend to stay silent while Robbi is working, but I realized something over the past couple of days while he's been writing out all these different reports and I think the stress is getting to him.

"I think you should slow down on that heavy workload Robbi," I said.

Robbi jumped out of his chair and clung to the bookshelf for his life.

"When did you get here?" He said.

I took a couple of steps toward his desk and placed my hands on the desk but when my fingers touched the wood they evaporated like leaving water out in a bottle for too long. I fixed my eyes on Robbi and said "I have always been here."

"I can't believe that you live in a world where mythical creatures exist, yet you're afraid of your own shadow that talks to you," I said as I switched his white lab coat out for the old gray hoodie in the photo.

Robbi's cell phone started going off, and a woman's face appeared on the surface of the phone. That was Valery. Her skin was a light mocha color and her hair was short, stopping at her shoulders. Robbi swiped down on the phone to answer the call and put it on speaker.

"Robbi hey, I just got a call from the chief," Valery said.

"Okay, what did she want?" Robbi said as he printed out the last of his report, sealing the papers in a large golden dim envelope. He put the envelope into a black leather bag and slung the bag over his shoulders.

"She said that a creature that was long lost has now surfaced and she needs us to go look for it," Valery said as her shoes squeaked with every step across the freshly mopped floor. She arrived at a dark red door that had a sign that read: Do Not Enter.

"Wait. Where are you right now Val?" Robbi said as a knock came on his office door.

I grabbed Robbi's Cannon Rebel camera with an SD card and charged the battery pack. Slipping them into his bag, he opened the door to see a woman wearing black pants, and a lilac purple t-shirt covered by a white lab coat. The name tag that hung from her coat collar read Valery.

"Chief also wants to tell us something and wants you and me to meet her at Level B3 in 30 minutes," Valery said, as she held two cups of coffee.

Robbi took one cup from her, took a sip of coffee, and said, "You do realize that nobody has ever been that far down to level B3 before?"

As the two walked down a flight of stairs, they came across one of their coworkers who had choppy golden hair wearing a red t-shirt covered by a white lab coat. His name tag read Jerry.

"Oh, if Mother 'N' wants to speak with you two on B3, then it's something really important.

She hasn't even told the elite team of research troops to handle the work." Jerry said.

Robbi and Valery both sipped their coffee.

"Well, he seems to be very knowledgeable. How does he know this before anyone?" I said. No one replied.

"I wonder if she might be asking for you two to take a deeper look into the incident that happened a month ago in the next town over, regarding the Cherry Bloom Inc. company." Jerry said as he opened a dark green door, followed them to an elevator, and pressed the down arrow for them.

The elevator door opened and Robbi stepped on before Valery got on with him. She stopped and asked Jerry a question.

"Why are you telling us this?"

Jerry smiled and said, "I'm just looking out for you two. I would hate for something bad to happen to one of you."

Valery didn't respond she stepped onto the elevator as Jerry waved to Robbi and her. The doors closed and the elevator descended.

There was a weird feeling in the air as we went deeper underground. It felt like an uneasiness of waves stirring under a boat before it capsizes over. Valery looked at Robbi. His eyes had rough bags forming under the eyelids. Robbi leaned on a metal rail to keep himself upright as he folded his arms.

"you haven't been sleeping the past 2 nights have you?" Valery asked.

Robbi looked at her narrowed eyes.

"What does it matter to you if I haven't slept in the

past couple of nights."

"Look I'm just worried about you and this isn't something you usually do?" She said.

I stood between Valery and Robbi as the elevator fluorescent light placed me on the center wall having Valery on my left and Robbi on my Right. Robbi rubbed the arch of his nose with his thumb and index finger.

"Robbi, look you have been taking on long hours and you need to get your rest. Val is just worried about her best friend." I said. The elevator started to shake as the box we were in slowed to nearly a complete stop.

"Look, Val, you wouldn't know what kind of stress I have been through. Working on report after report and then pulling all-nighters on top of that." He said as he took a couple of steps toward Valery.

Valery tightened her hand into a fist. She grew impatient, knowing that something didn't feel right with the way her partner was acting.

"Come on Robbi, we're both in the same boat here. We both have the same amount of work stacked up for us. You just need to get your mind in the right headspace." She said.

Robbi snapped as he lashed out at Valery in anger. He kept pushing his index finger into Valery's chest.

"I bet all you do is sit at your desk and work for a little bit then goof off the rest of the time," Robbi said.

Just then, Valery's fist flew and slammed into Robbi's face. The sound was like wood being smashed on concrete as her fist connected with his face right between his eyes.

Robbi buried his face in his hands as he staggered backward. Tears started to form in Valery's eyes out of frustration.

"Don't you ever say that about me? I'm your friend first and partner second. Don't get it twisted." Valery said. The elevator door opened and she walked out onto a checkerboard floor down a long hallway, only to arrive at a large double stainless steel door.

I stood next to Valery as I took the form of Robbi but looked like a cloud of smoke. I looked at her and wiped some tears out of her eyes.

"What are we here for again?" I said to Valery as she pulled her phone out of her pocket. A picture of a crimson bird flashed on her screen. The way the photo was taken, I could tell that it was some type of bird but it was too blurry as it looked like smoke trailed behind it.

Robbi stepped out of the elevator still holding his face only to realize the situation he just put himself in with his partner Valery.

WHAT'S IN THE BOX

A house party is going on in an old run-down hotel. Chatter can be heard upstairs in the kitchen as the adults are having a good time joking with each other and clinking their wine glasses. Beethoven was playing on the radio as the sound was muffled from under the floorboards. Two young children were walking down into the basement, a boy named Nix and a girl named Brook. As the two crept further down the steps, Brook clung tightly to Nix's arm.

"Hey... are you sure it's okay for us to be down here without any of the adults knowing?" Brook asked Nix.

He didn't respond as they drew closer to a black, steel door

"What are you getting nervous for?" Nix questioned his friend.

Brook laughed nervously and shook her head as they both pushed with all of their might, but the door didn't even budge. Brook pouted and looked at Nix, "What are we going to do now?"

Nix looked at the door and yelled, "STUPID DOOR!" He kicked the door hurting his foot in the process. The door opened just a little for the kids to squeeze themselves through. Once they were inside, the room had boxes that filled up to the ceiling and as far back as the room could go. Brook briefly glided her fingers across the books on the old shelf. The books then fell to the ground from the dry rotted shelves with a series of loud thumps causing the string binding that was wrapped around the books to fall apart. A pearl blue rectangular chest-shaped box with un-recognizable engraved letters sat in the middle of what appeared to be an endless room to the kids. "This place is awesome, Brook, we can use this as our secret base!" Nix said in amazement as Brook looked at the box and tilted her head. She said to Nix, "Um… That doesn't look right…"

"What are you talking about, Brook?" Nix asked her. Then, he walked closer to the box and saw his full name on the lip of the box in big black letters, "NIX INA LTE". Purple smoke drooled out of the box and crawled to the children giving them a chill down their spines. They ran for the door as it closed, cutting the kids off from their normal lives.

Then, the door opened, and all Brook and Nix saw was a room of never-ending darkness.

Nix's hand wrapped tightly around Brook's hand as fear filled the kids. The chest shook violently causing the kids to turn. Brook and Nix stared wide-eyed as the box rampaged in their direction knocking lose all the books and boxes laid across the floor. The box opened up to show sharp teeth around its lip. Two black shadow arms emerged from the mouth of the chest, wrapping their slen-der fingers around the kids' legs as they tighten on their ankles and yanked them back.

They let out a horrifying scream, and when they re-open their eyes, the chest was gone.

THE OVERSEERS OF JACOB

If you think the story you're about to hear is one of some great knights who goes off to a distant land to conquer a few quests and slay a mighty dragon, I'm sorry but no, this is not one of those stories. This is a story of a man and how he is trying to figure out his life while searching for the right direction to go towards. This man's name was Jacob, and he had a low buzz-cut hairstyle. He wore blue jeans, a light blue t-shirt that read "Inspire to be Inspired", and black converse shoes.

On this chilly spring day, Jacob stood outside of his College University gate and stared at a large banner that hung over the University entrance, which read in big white letters "Welcome New Students." The letters were plastered onto a dark blood red background fabric that was being held by two thick white strings. Jacob's hands started to sweat as something in his stomach turned to jelly. Other new students started to walk casually onto campus. They passed Jacob who still stood motionless at the gate entrance. Jacob inhaled and let out a shaky breath as he took one step through the gate.

"Okay time for me to start a new chapter in my life," said Jacob.

As he was on the other side of the gate, he saw tall buildings made from red stone bricks that varied in unusual sizes. The buildings that Jacob looked at all had engravings on the brick pillar outside the door to show what the building would be used for. One building had a dim orange rooftop with an engraving that resembled an artist's paintbrush. What stood out to Jacob was not the fact that the buildings had different icons engraved on the side of the pillar on the entrance of the building next to the door, but it was some of the people who were entering certain sections of the buildings who looked like they shouldn't be going in there. Through the door that the students entered was nothing but darkness, but no students walked out to leave.

"Maybe these other departments are hosting some sort of get-together to try and get us new students into different places to get new members," Jacob muttered.

He continued walking past the different department buildings and came into a large circular space where two sets of stairs on either side of the circle showed as the entrance and exit. All around the circle were a bunch of tables and tents. Posters were plastered and taped up informing new students how to join different clubs, sports, fraternities and sororities, or other extracurricular activities on the wild campus college.

See, with this college, not only on the first day was their new freshman but there were also foreigners from other countries who wanted to attend this amazing college. I could not tell you why they chose this college to save my life. All I know is that this is where I had my encounter with our "hero" of the story and at first, I didn't know what to make of him. I guess this was only because I needed to get to know who this guy was first before I made any rash judgment calls. That's usually what happens when it comes to me and meeting someone—whether that be a client for work or trying to make a new friend. I sometimes follow this old saying, "don't uncover a book without reading it." No, I don't think that was it. Oh, I remember how it went it was "Don't judge a book by its cover." Yeah that was it.

Everywhere I looked was crowded. People were all over the place trying to get pressured into joining a club or something. Some guy was wearing a bright orange shirt that read "Taco's every Tuesday" in black letters. He had a large tan sombrero sitting next to him as he sat at a table. The sign on the table read, "Join the Spanish club". This was something I was not up for, so I decided to keep pushing my way through the sea of students to see what the next club had to offer. As I kept moving through people some random person slammed their elbow into my back and another person tripped me up knocking me to the ground.

"Hey, watch where you're going!" I said.

I slowly picked myself up from the cold ground and dusted off my old, green hoodie. The weird thing is that I didn't know that the person I was about to run into was the guy I had been watching from time to time. But let me tell you now, I am not a stalker, and I don't want you to think... "Oh no that's exactly what it sounds like?"

That's not what I need you to think because that's not how it was. The person I bumped into was a guy who had a light blue t-shirt and blue jeans.

"Oh, I'm sorry man I didn't mean to bump into you," Jacob said.

I looked at him as I was still brushing off the dirt from my clothes.

"No man, it's not your fault. You know there's just a lot of people here." I said.

When I looked at this guy, I did not realize until I laid eyes on this person who was in front of me that this dude had one hazel brown eye and one light blue eye. What I found interesting about this guy's blue eye was that it felt like I was looking out at the vast clear blue ocean. So, I decided to introduce myself to this man who was still looking at me as we were still being pushed around by the other students.

"Hey there, my name is Allen. It's nice to meet you?" I said.

I held out my hand to offer a handshake, but at first, he didn't take the handshake. He looked like he was staring off into space, but when he looked down at my hand stretched out, it was like for some reason that's what brought him back to reality.

"Oh, yeah, hi. I'm Jacob. It's nice to meet you as well." Jacob said.

He grasped my hand with a firm shake. Jacob and I made our way to a large square building that looked to be a lounging space for students who wanted to take a break from being asked so many questions about joining clubs.

"Okay let's see where a good place for us would be to talk?" I said.

We both looked around on the first floor, but it seemed like all the tables and couches were full. Jacob and I gave one another a worried glance and took an elevator to the second floor of the building. As we rode up to the second floor, I couldn't help but think to myself, *I hope I can give him the right push in the direction he needs to go.* I looked at Jacob and he looked like he was getting nervous.

"Hey, Jacob do you like card games?" I said.

His ears perked up when I said card games.

"Yeah, I love card games. Which ones are your favorite Allen? I like speed." Jacob said.

"Oh, really I favor the card game war," I said.

Jacob let out a chuckle. I looked at him nervously only because I didn't know what was so funny to him. The elevator doors opened to the second floor and that's when we saw some pool tables and a few foosball tables. As a lot of empty rooms that I guessed were used for studying or for friends to hang out with one another. I saw that there was a room in the far back with what looked to be one table and two booth seats on either side of the table. I gestured over to Jacob.

"Jacob, why don't we try to find a booth," I said.

We looked around in the different rooms. I thought that the rooms were empty but they slowly started to fill up with people. We kept looking. Jacob cupped his hands around his eyes and saw a room in the back of the second-floor study room.

"I can see a room. It looks like the second room on the right is open," Jacob said.

As the two of us hurried our way past the other rooms, which seemed to be turned into conference rooms, I figured the rooms allowed students to get work done or conduct business-like meetings with close friends about class or good times to meet up during the school semester. I don't know why but I think depending on how this semester goes for Jacob it should lessen the amount of paperwork that I'm going to have to do when I get back to my job.

Jacob and I approached the room on the second floor. We looked through the wide window and saw a girl sitting in one of the booths reading a book on how to write a stage play. The girl wore a white t-shirt and blue jeans. She had a warm red jacket that had been lying next to her. This girl's hair was a dark shade of violet and tied up in a ponytail. Her skin was a tan white; the color of a peach. When she looked up from her book, her eyes were that of a soft green as her gaze landed on me.

She waved at me, and I waved back.

"There you are?" the girl said.

When she said this, I pointed at myself and looked around to see if she was talking to anyone else. I looked back at her, and she nodded at me as I made my way into the room, and she slid the book she was reading.

"Where have you been Allen?" she said.

"Sorry, I got caught up in a sea of students outside," I said.

Jacob slowly walked into the study room and the girl looked at him.

"Who is this person, Allen?" she said.

I walked over to Jacob and threw my right arm around him.

"This is my friend Jacob. I just met him," I said.

When I had my arm around Jacob's shoulder, I could feel him shaking because I think he was nervous. I think the reason why Jacob was feeling so nervous was that there were now two people in a room with him who knew each other but he didn't know either of them. Other than me, whom he had just met.

Jacob looked up at the girl and rubbed his shaky arm to try and calm himself down. He had calmed down a little as he looked at the girl nervously and waved at her.

"Hello, my name is Jacob. It's nice to meet you?" Jacob said.

The girl looked at me, then at Jacob, and pointed at him while mouthing to me *That's him?* I nodded at her as I pulled a deck of playing cards out of my backpack.

I took a seat in the booth next to the girl as Jacob just stood at the edge of the table.

"I hope you don't mind us sitting in the booth with you, do you?" I said.

Jacob reached out his hand and was a little scared to say something but suddenly spoke up.

"Hey, Allen, I don't think it would be a good idea to just occupy a space that someone else already has. We should just leave." Jacob said.

I looked at the girl and she closed her book and gave me an annoyed look.

"Oh, no it's fine you guys can sit here with me. I was just waiting for someone to show up anyway." May said.

I took the playing cards out of their packaging and tried to take out the wild joker card and started to deal out the cards between Jacob and myself.

"May, would you like to play a card game with Jacob and me?" I said.

May shrugged and place the book she was reading in her bag. She leaned on the table and looked at me with a look of competitiveness in her eyes.

"Sure, what kind of card game are we playing?" May asked.

I glanced at Jacob as I continued to give out the cards among the three of us. May and Jacob started to collect the cards that I had given to them.

"Well, the game Jacob likes to play is the game speed, but that's not the case," I said.

Jacob let out a laugh as he studied his cards to see what he had.

"The game we're playing, you two, is war," I said.

May looked at her cards and then glanced up at me.

"Wait why did you decide that we would play the game of war?" May asked.

"Well, I chose this game or war because it kind of has to do with strategy. This is going to be an interesting game we're playing." I said.

As we started to play our game, May had this tic about her. For May, it felt more like an itch that needed to be scratched. She was very competitive, and she did not like to lose. So, it looked like May was trying to catch Jacob off guard with a little small talk.

"So, Jacob, mind if I ask you something?" May said.

"Go ahead and take your shot," Jacob said.

"What's your major?" May asked.

"Well for my major, I had decided on it being Theater. I figured I would be able to do something in acting with the help of theater," Jacob said.

"Now that's interesting to hear. What about you May? What's your major?" I asked.

May had placed three hearts on the small pile of cards that we had in the center of the table.

"If you guys must know, my major is business," May said.

"Okay. Why business?" Jacob asked.

"Well, my family is trying to start up their own business and they would like for me to at least know how everything in the business world works," May said.

The game started to get intense because it got to a point where Jacob and I had drawn the same number.

"I declare war." Jacob and I said.

We both had to draw four cards and when it came to the fifth card, we had to reveal who had the highest number. Sadly, the number I drew was five clubs and the card Jacob drew was seven diamonds. I had to give him the pile of cards he just won, and the man was stacking up quite the hale of cards.

The game continued slowly at first and it felt like the three of us had started to get to know each other. In this sense for me, even though I had just listened to the conversations that happened between the three of us, it felt like a true friendship started to form that linked all of us together.

"I know this is going to sound like a weird question, but I have to ask?" Jacob said.

"Oh, and what's this question you want me and Allen to answer?" May said.

"The thing I would like to know is how do you know Allen?" Jacob asked.

My right hand twitched as it lay on the table.

"What are you talking about? Why would you think that May and I know each other?" I asked.

"To be honest, the entire time we have been playing this little game, the two of you have been silent as if you two know something," Jacob said.

May and I looked at each other and she shook her head letting out a sigh.

"Jacob, see the reason why Allen and I know each other is because we are old friends. We had both gone to the same high school," May said.

Jacob had placed his card on the table and then leaned in close to me.

I had started to sweat a little bit. I felt like I could not tell Jacob the truth as to how May and I knew each other.

There was one thought that came to my mind: if I screw this up, the higher-ups *will have my head.*

"Is what May said true: that you and she knew each other back in High School?" Jacob asked.

I had to get a hold of my nerves before I would give him my answer.

"Look Jacob, what my friend May here is saying is all true. The two of us went to the same High School. She got very competitive when we played dodgeball back then." I said.

After I told him that, I felt my heartbeat slow down and no longer ring in my ears. I wiped my sweaty hands off my jeans.

As I tried to get us to resume our game, May stated something that I didn't think I would hear.

"Jacob, what are your thoughts on destiny?" May said.

Jacob placed one of his cards on the new pile of cards that had been started.

"What do you mean by destiny? Like trying to determine one's fate?" Jacob asked.

May looked down at the table as if she was deep in thought.

"I'm talking about how a person would go about moving through life. Like would you want to live your life on your terms or would you rather have someone else dictate to you how your life is supposed to go?" May said.

I was caught off guard by May saying something as random as that. There are times when I have no clue what she's thinking most of the time. She can throw me for a loop with some of the stuff she says, but I think she has means of doing things to figure out what she needs to know.

Jacob scratched his chin as he placed another card down.

"Well, I think that if it were me, I think that I would want to live my own life on my terms. I feel like that would be better than having another person telling me how I should live." Jacob said.

I looked around the room and the door that Jacob and I had entered was gone for some reason. The room started to grow darker. The darkness encroached on us slowly. The table grew brighter as the room started getting dimmer. Some of the darkness that was pushed back made its way into May's body like someone had pinched her as she rubbed her arm.

"Jacob, when you get a chance, you should look behind you," I said.

Our game continued and then May looked up from her cards and saw the same thing that I had seen with the darkness encroaching on us. She looked at me and placed a card down.

"You know sometimes there are moments when a person holds so much information that they want to tell someone who they just met everything about who they are," May said.

As May spoke these words, I tried to keep a calm facial expression even though in my mind I was freaking out. *May what are you saying? This is not the time to try and explain to him who we truly are.* I thought.

So, I know that most people don't know who May and I are, and I don't think it's my place to say so I feel like I should just let May say what we are.

Jacob had placed another card down on the pile as the number of cards in his hand started to decrease.

"May what are you talking about?" Jacob asked.

I looked at May and whispered "Do you think what you're about to say is truly going to help him in the long run?"

"Well no. I just think that if we tell Jacob the fact that we are angels, maybe just maybe he will believe us, and we can help move him towards the goal he wants to achieve." May said.

"Hey, when we are done here, Allen, you and I need to head to the rooftop of the music building, I need to talk to you in private." May told me as I started to get another uneasy feeling but decided to ignore it.

Okay look I know that what she is saying is true and that maybe Jacob just might be able to believe us. What I feel uneasy about is the possibility of him not believing us. It's not like I have any proof to show him.

"Allen do you know what May is talking about?" Jacob said.

"Jacob this is going to sound crazy but, do you ever feel like you're being watched? Like you feel a person's eye gazes in your direction but every time you turn around to see who was looking at you there would be no one there. Then you decide to go on with your business only to later feel another glance at you. Only for the same thing to happen once again, you turn around and nobody is there?" I asked.

Jacob thought about what I had asked him as he placed another card down.

"Now that you mention it yeah, I do feel like that sometimes," Jacob said.

I leaned on the table and looked at Jacob.

"Would you like to know why that is?" I said.

Jacob looked at me then back at May and shrugged his shoulders.

"Sure, I'll ask why the situation like that is," Jacob said.

May cleared her throat.

"The reason why you feel like someone is watching you is that the person, or should I say people, who are keeping an eye on you is us," May said.

She pointed from herself to me to show Jacob that she was talking about me and her. When Jacob looked behind him at the door, he saw that the door was still there and to him, everything looked normal. Jacob leaned back in the booth and just looked at May and me.

"Okay let's say I believe you, what happens now?" Jacob said.

"Well since our game is about to come to an end, here's what's going to happen. You, Jacob, are going to walk out of this study room and off to your classes just like every other student on this campus. May and I will continue to look out for you to see how you navigate through your life." I said.

"Now this doesn't mean that we will be gone. The two of us will still be around just watching you from a safe distance. Oh, don't worry, we can all get together some days and just play card games. I enjoyed this game we should play it again." May said.

Jacob nodded in agreement as he walked out of the study room and to his class in the Theater department. May and I collected all the cards and ended up using a campus map to find our way around to the different classes that Jacob had.

As we walked over to the music building and ascended the winding spiral staircase, we came to a large grey door. I opened the door and to May's surprise, we were met with a blinding white light as the sun hit our faces. We walked out on the rocky loose gravel beneath our feet. I leaned on the guarded railing as I looked out at the big blue sky that seemed to stretch for miles.

"What did you want to talk about?" I said.

May walked toward me and she embraced me in a hug.

"Hey, do you think we made the right choice?" May asked.

"Yeah, I think we did," I said.

A couple of tears started to fall onto my hoodie from May crying as she placed her hands on my chest.

"Great. I'm glad. Sorry, it has to end like this." May said.

"What are you talk-" I said.

With one push before I knew it, I was falling from to the side of the building as I looked up at May. For a brief second, I felt the dark presence once again, but this time it was coming off May's body as if she was engulfed by black flames.

LIFE AND FILM

Okay, so I want to try my best to tell you this. Sometimes I wonder what a person's life or even your life is like through the lens of a camera. I mean the thought of life is like a camera and seeing the world through the eyes of another. I feel like it would be cool to see the waves of a salty blue ocean or even to stand at the top of a mountain and overlook the town below.

That sure must be nice for others instead of being stuck in a cold room surrounded by a mountain of books and documents to sift through. I've been locked in this room for a couple of years. I don't know, at this point all the days kind of blur together. I hope I can find the answer to the question of what it means to live.

I have this gray cement-colored file sitting on my cherry oak desk and I see that you and your fellow companions have traveled through different worlds and observed many different lives. It says in this file that you have seen a confrontation between two supernatural beings and other things that I'm not going to get into now. It must be nice to be able to overlook other realms and place an imaginary version of yourself in a fictional world and leave the world of issues and problems behind.

Oh, wait where are my manners? This must seem so out of order listening to a man whose name you don't even know. My apologies, ghosts. Well, I call you ghosts because that's what you appear to me as. Even though I have no clue as to how you got into my workplace in the basement of CBI (Cherry Bloom Inc.), that's beside the point. My name is Ryan, and I work as this company's archivist. But can I be honest with you? I mean right now it's just me sitting at my desk in a cluttered room. Don't mind the papers. I have a friend who is the head of the company and the weird thing is that she is always wearing red.

What's interesting is, your file says that you guys had encountered someone wearing red back in your previous journey before you ended up in this office. This place, okay I should say this room, feels like a prison cell. I can't leave unless higher-ups tell me I can leave and most of my food is delivered and left at the door of the basement. There, next to the wooden bookshelf is a long metal shoot for me to receive my mail.

There was a knocking on my door and the mechanical lock opened from the outside as a blinding white light from the fluorescent lights bounced off the bleak cement wall and back to my face. I could see the outline of a person who had long black hair, like no stars in the sky kind of black. This person was a woman, and her eyes were emerald that shined like gemstones. She wore a long red jacket with the letters CBI in the upper right corner of the jacket.

"Greetings, Ryan. How are you doing today?" said the woman with a smile.

"I'm all right Nyx. What is it that you need? You usually don't come down here unless you need something. So, what is it?" I said.

"What? I can't come down to see how my brother is?" Nyx said.

I didn't say anything in response because even though she says that I'm her brother, we are not related by blood or even adopted. We are friends, and just act like siblings, it's awkward but that's how we got to know each other. Now, Nyx is the owner of Cherry Bloom Inc. I think the person who is writing my story could have just called the company Sakura which translates to cherry blossom in Japanese, but that's not my point.

"I need the reports from last month so I can make sure everything looks good for our next group of clients," Nyx said.

I looked at the floor and noticed a cardboard box that was organized with different clients' problems within it. I didn't think much about it and just handed Nyx the box. Well, I slid the box over to her. Nyx knelt to pick up the box when something clattered to the floor. When I looked to see what hit the ground there was something that resembles the form of a T.V. remote with two pointed needles sticking out from its top like a taser.

I was about to tell Nyx that she had dropped something but by the time I opened my mouth she had already slipped the taser back into her pocket.

"Thanks for these and try not to work too hard," Nyx said as she left, and the door locked behind her all on its own.

I continued going through different case files when I heard something hit my wooden floor. It was a stack of superhero comics and old college textbooks that had hit the ground. What I wasn't expecting was to see a little girl rubbing her head from slamming headfirst into those books. I screamed and ran to my phone which was a land-line that would only call Nyx.

"State who you are, or I will call security," I said as I placed the phone up to my ear only to not hear a busy tone. I could hear the sound of whimpers on the other line, and before the line was cut, I heard a frightened female voice whimper, "Help…Me." as the line was cut to empty silence.

"Wait, this girl means no harm. Put the phone down and I will explain everything," a voice said.

I looked at the girl and she looked to be no older than ten years old. She had bright blue eyes like the sky on a cloudless day. Her lips didn't move.

I pointed at her.

"Did you just say that?" I said and the girl shook her head.

She had a bracelet on that switched colors from blue to purple and ended up velvet red.

"No, this child didn't say that. I did," said the Bracelet.

I was taken aback by this. To think that this kind of Hi-tech existed in this company.

"Wait, hold up. You can talk?" I asked the bracelet.

"Yes," the Bracelet answered.

"Who are you then Bracelet?" I asked.

"I am an AI life form created to protect this child. I'm called Velvet. You are going to have to name this child and take care of her," Velvet said.

Great, now I must take care of a kid and care not only for my own life but two others as well. This was an unusual turn of events. My roll of film has just doubled in length.

I looked at the girl.

"What did you first go by before you ended up in this room?" I said.

She pointed at her throat and held up an X with her arms.

"This child is mute and cannot speak," Velvet said.

I handed the girl a notebook and a black sharp marker. I wrote a message in the book to see how we can talk.

Use this notebook to ask me any questions you may have. What do you want me to call you?

"She was originally called case number 0021," Velvet said.

The girl wrote something down in the notebook. Her handwriting was shaky and messy, but I was able to make out what she wanted to say.

(Kid)

I don't like being called by a number.

"Okay so you don't like that name then. How about Sora?" I asked as the girl's eyes sparkled with joy and she wrote another message.

"Sora, I like that one. What does it mean?"

"Well, Sora means sky," I said.

"Sora and I are here because we escaped a lab experiment where researchers were trying to put people into dreams and have them face their nightmares. But the intention was to have the nightmares win the fight and possess the physical body to give the nightmare a truly human form." Velvet said.

This isn't what I was expecting to hear about Nyx's company.

Over the course of three weeks, Velvet explained to me how Sora and her escaped and found their way into my office. I found an old pack of playing cards in my desk drawer, so Sora and I played go-fish as well as the game war. There was a pizza box that came down the main shoot. I opened up the box and there was half of a pepperoni pizza left in there. The half a pie was smashed against the lid of the box looking uneatable until Sora tore off a slice and eat it.

"Is it good?" I said.

Sora gave me a thumbs up letting me know it was safe to eat the pie.

I started to feel like a real bond had formed between Sora and Myself.

After I got all the information from Velvet about what happened to her and Sora, I had Sora help me out with organizing papers and moving boxes. In a way, Sora became my assistant and made my work go a lot faster than when it was just me. The only problem was the more time I spent with Sora. I started to feel weak like my strength was leaving quickly.

Suddenly there was a knock at the door. I told Sora to go hide behind a box pyramid that was at my desk.

The door opened on its own as usual.

"Hi, Nyx is everything all right?" I said.

"I need to speak with you in my office. Bring anyone else you have in your office with you," Nyx said.

"Ryan are you okay? You look pale." Nyx said.

"Yeah, I'm fine. Just hard trying to sleep with all this work I have to get done," I lied.

After Nyx left, I packed a bag for Sora and gave her my old black leather jacket. We walked out the door and down a long narrow hallway and ended up at an elevator. Once in, I looked at Sora as I helped her put on my black jacket.

"Velvet, can I ask you something? Can you make a digital clone of Sora so I can trick Nyx into thinking she is with me," I said?

"Sure, but are you not coming with us?" Velvet said.

"Sadly no, I will not be going. I must confront this boss on my own. Hopefully, I can talk some sense into her." I said.

The elevator stopped on the first floor and the doors opened. I knelt to look Sora in the eyes.

"Everything is going to be okay, just head to the entrance and the two of you are home free," I said as I hugged Sora and tears dripped onto my shirt.

As Sora and Velvet left, I felt heartbroken because of what I was about to go through when I met Nyx. It meant that I would never get to see Sora again. I just hope her film journey will last a lot longer than I have.

I think I know what it means to live. Not just for oneself, but for others and to make a difference in that person's life.

The elevator reached the top floor, and I stepped out and confronted Nyx as she sat at her desk looking at me.

"Welcome, Ryan. Glad you could make it. Do you have any idea what you have done?" Nyx said.

"I saved a kid's life and I'm okay with that," I said.

"I don't think you get it, Ryan. That thing you call a 'kid' is a monster!"

"That's no way to talk about a child Nyx. She needed help even though she couldn't speak, so I helped her."

"Case number 0021 is not to be trusted. What is with you?"

Two wolves walked out from behind Nyx's desk growling at me as she got up from her seat and walked toward me.

"She isn't case number 0021. Her name is Sora and she's a good person." I said.

Nyx started laughing.

"Oh, that's sweet and you even gave it a name," Nyx said still laughing.

The office phone rang, and a voice came over the speaker.

"Hi, Nyx. it's Chestnut. I need to run the numbers with you to make sure everything is good for project surrealist. Those two candidates you wanted me to investigate, Sam and Mary, they don't suspect a thing." Chestnut said.

"Chestnut, I'll call you back at another time, I'm in the middle of some family issues," Nyx said staring at me.

Both dogs rushed me from the left and the right. When I tried to move my feet, they were stuck in place. The dog on my left side took a bite into my leg and I heard my bone snap. I screamed out as I was flooded with pain.

"I treated you like family Ryan, and this is what I get?" Nyx said.

"Family, huh,? You sure have a funny way with words. Families don't leave other family members in a basement for years on end." I said as the other dog took a bite out of my left arm.

I lay on the cold ground as my vision started switching from clear to blurry. I saw Nyx standing over me.

"Well, you don't know my family," Nyx said.

I saw her take out the same taser she had before. She almost looked sad. She knelt to me and the last thing I heard her say was.

"You showed so much promise. Why did you have to grow a backbone and not listen."

When I awoke, I was submerged in a tank of water, but Nyx was nowhere to be seen. On the other side of the glass, I saw a child with dark chocolate skin being hooked up to medical equipment. He looked to be around the same age as Sora.

SURREAL DREAMS

ave you ever had a dream that felt very real to you? Then for some reason, you could not explain why when you told someone you know. This was the case that increased with Mary every time she went to sleep. While sleeping, Mary would be swept away from her apartment bedroom to an unknown world. The only time that Mary realized she was awake was when in the dream world if she was critically injured from something attacking or falling from a high place with the thought that she might die. Dreams come from our subconscious given form.

One cold October morning, Mary wore blue jeans, black high-top converse, and a black t-shirt covered by a large gray hoodie that had fur on the inside to keep her warm. Mary had short black hair that stopped at her shoulders. She walked to the nearest coffee shop on the grounds of her university along with her friend Sam who had messy brown hair. He wore blue jeans, sneakers and a black leather jacket that read on the back *Dreams are in the clouds while Reality takes us back down to Earth.* Sam rubbed his hazel brown eyes to try and wake himself up.

"Why do we have to get up so early in the morning for this class," said Sam as he yawned.

Mary looked at him "Hey you didn't have to sign up for the 8a.m. class like I did to take this Phycology class."

The two of them arrived at the Rolling Bean Coffee shop where Mary ordered a regular coffee. The scent of roasted coffee beans filled the air of the little shop as Mary and Sam sat in a small red booth while their order got prepared. Sam crossed his arms on the table and placed his chin over his arms.

"So, do you know what we are even doing in class today?" said Mary as she took out a dark purple notebook from her black bag and started jotting down ideas for a story she had in the works.

"I don't know. Professor Chestnut said something last time about wanting to do an experimental lecture on the state of dreams," Sam said as his eyes looked up at Mary from the maple wood table. She kept her pen moving on the paper like an unrelenting wave of words crashing down on a sandy beach.

"Sam and Mary," a barista called out. As Mary and Sam retrieved their beverages and opened two glass double doors into the freezing air, Mary and Sam both took a sip of their coffee.

"I am so glad I got this to warm up my bones," Sam said.

They continued to walk on the cold concrete with every step feeling like icicle needles as the air hit their skin. They came upon a brick building with a brain and an open book engraved over the door.

Going into the building, the pair walked into a large conference room that was in the shape of a circle. In the center of the room was a man with light brown hair. Little streaks of gray could be seen. He was wearing a creamy peanut butter suit with a dark purple tie. Their professor looked like a human-size PB&J without the bread. There were only ten students in Professor Chestnut's class.

One student in an orange hoodie raised his hand, "Um, Professor are you having other people come in during your lecture?"

As Professor Chestnut set up two metal folding chairs on either side of a solid wooden podium. There was a small T.V. that sat on the podium in between the two chairs. He cleared his throat.

"Yes, other students, as well as faculty, will be dropping in on our class to witness traveling through dreams."

Sam leaned toward Mary who was on his right "Does he think we are going to figure out how dreams work?" Mary shrugged.

"Sam and Mary, can I use you two as examples for this experiment," Professor Chestnut asked as they sat down in the two chairs. Chestnut hooked them up to a monitor on the T.V. screen that showed three screens. One was a map of Sam and Mary's dream world. The second was a screen that monitored their brain waves and heart activity. The last one showed only static snow as Chestnut could only look at one person's dream at a time. He went with Sam, first. Chestnut gave Sam and Mary, knockout gas as they went limp and slumped over in their chairs.

As the rest of the students watched their two classmates drift off to sleep, they all said in unison "Whoa!"

One student raised her hand and said "excuse me Professor, don't you think it would have been better for Sam and Mary to have signed a waver or something before putting them through this?"

Chestnut continued to work with the machine that Sam and Mary were hooked up to, and said "everything is going to be fine. I think one of them signed the waver."

Chestnut turned back to the subjects, speaking to their sleeping bodies, "You should only be knocked out for 30 minutes. That can give you time to explore and come back."

When Mary woke up, she was in a flush green meadow that felt like wax paper in her hands. She looked up to see the sky was a teal blue as if someone had carefully used a paintbrush to map out how her sky looked with no clouds in sight. Off in the distance, Mary saw a weeping willow tree sitting on top of a hill with red leaves instead of their usual green. As Mary walked towards the hill, blue roses formed at her feet and lit up her path to the tree. Once she made it, she realized that the weeping willow was crying as a huge tear drop fell from one of the willow's branches and showered Mary in seawater.

"Okay, well, that was unexpected," said Mary as she tried to shake herself dry, but her clothes stayed soaked.

She wrung out some of the water from her hair and saw a child in a dark red hoodie and black jeans. The hood was up so she could not see the child's eyes.

"Who are you?" Mary said puzzled as the kid looked up at her grinning to show his shiny white teeth.

Mary covered her eyes to shield herself from the blinding light of the child as he turned away from her and walked through the willow tree disappearing from Mary's sight.

"Hey, wait, kid don't go," Mary said as a bright red door appeared at the foot of the tree. She stepped through to fall into what felt like a never-ending darkness. Bright Orange torches illuminated below Mary as the view exploded with a crimson red color that the sky became. All around her were large stone red pyramids as pillars of fire blocked the gate entrance of the pyramids, leaving the steps untouched. The same little kid, but in a black leather jacket, ascended one of the pyramid steps as their light violet hair swayed in the wind.

"You're not supposed to be here," the kid said to Mary as she floated next to the kid as they continued to climb the steps.

"What do you mean? Where are we anyway," she said.

The child let out a sigh as they looked at Mary.

"Do I have to spell it out for you?" the child asked.

As Mary looked at the child, she realized that the child had soft tan paper mashie-like skin and the hair covered only the right side of the child's face. On the left side of Mary, she noticed that the child's left eye was creamy milky white.

"You are in a dream," the child started to say.

The temperature in the place started to increase as Mary started to feel her body heat up as if she had a high fever. Mary's body started to peal as her skin burst into flames as she tried to let out a scream only for no sound to escape her lips. Her scene transitioned from a fiery pit to being in an endless white room with two figures in the distance making their way over to her.

As the two figures approached Mary and came clear into view, she saw how small they were. When the two small figures stood before Mary, one was a little boy in a dark red hoodie and the other was a girl with violet hair that sparkled like gemstones in a cave. She wore a black jacket that was too big for her.

"Who are you two? What do you mean? I'm not supposed to be here," Mary said.

The two kids looked at each other. The boy looked back at Mary "I'm Ben," said the boy in the red hoodie.

"I'm Summer. But look, we don't have time for this," said the girl in the black jacket.

"Summer's right. We were sent into your dreams by a person named Nyx and there are two ways you're getting out of this," Ben said.

Ben held out a black hilt of a golden blade towards Mary.

"Either we kill you and that takes you back into your world, or have one of us live your life for you, but you will be living from the backseat, not in control of your actions," Ben said as Mary took the sword from him.

"Wait! Kill you? You two didn't do anything wrong," Mary said.

"I don't see an exit anywhere, do you? Besides, we won't die. All you have to do is hit us in the chest" Summer said.

"So do I have to fight you one-on-one?" Mary asked as she studied the blade.

"No, you will just have to see," Ben said as he grabbed Summer's hand, and both were engulfed in a flash of dim white light.

A dark-gray female figure stepped out of the light and stood where Ben and Summer were standing. The female had long purple hair with red streaks throughout. She doubled over in pain as long black needles shot out from her back and started taking on the form of spider legs. As the female got raised into the air she opened her four eyes, the first two milky white and the second two pitch black.

"Oh, this isn't good," Mary said as the mutant spider figure charged at her.

Mary met her opponent head-on as she charged at the creature. The creature threw out three large needles from within a black jacket that fit her. They flew at Mary as she dodged, sliding under the needles. One tiny splinter shot out and grazed Mary's arm as she drove the golden blade into the chest of the creature. The creature shrieked out in pain as she leaped for Mary pinning her to the ground.

"You can't leave us here," the creature said as one of her spider legs pierced through Mary's chest.

Mary's eyes flew open as she woke up back in her Phycology class drenched in sweat.

"I shouldn't have signed that waiver. Man, that was rough," Mary muttered to herself as a woman in a red jacket got up and left the lecture room catching Mary's eye.

"Hey, are you all right Mary?" Sam asked as Mary grabbed his hand and rushed out the door to find the woman in the red jacket.

THE CONTAGIOUS AND CHAOTIC VIRUS

In an underground laboratory, a scientist by the name of Don Rah and his team had come up with a serum that they thought would be able to combat contagious disease from spreading at its source. The Government had put a lot of money upfront to keep this major science experiment sealed tight.

Don knew that this virus serum injection test would make or break his career as a well-known scientist in his field. This disease that Don and his team were tasked with fighting was something that was kind of like cancer but not quite. Instead of the cells going into a more dormant state returning to a normal blood cell and going back to the natural flow of how the body should work, this disease would continue to stay in the host's body making some of the cells go through a combustion phase as the body rives in pain. The government referred to this top secret study as Serum X.

"Will this serum work, Dr. Rah?" Asked an Army General.

As Don was flipping through a binder overlooking how the injection was supposed to work and checking for any backup plans to shut down the experiment. He looked up from his notes and said: "Well...yes General. In theory, it should work if nothing goes wrong."

"In theory, Dr. Rah we don't have time for you and your theories. You do realize that if this 'X' serum doesn't work then I will be forced to put you out of the job. right?" said General Mason.

Mason roared over a loudspeaker into the observation room as he stood behind bulletproof glass.

"All right, Dr. Rah we are ready for the test." stated one of the other researchers as a female test subject comes into the room and laid on the operation table. Don and other researchers on his team safely restrained the female patient and inject a blue vile filled with the X Serum into the neck of the subject.

"Okay the subject is stable and it seems like the virus is working," Don said as he looked at a computer that was monitoring the woman's vitals.

"Dr. Rah, the subject appears to be in the clear and I think we did it. The disease doesn't seem to be in her-" a female researcher started to say as she got cut off.

Sirens started to blare out in warning as something seemed to be going wrong with the experiment. The subject's body started to shake and flail about as the straps that were held to keep her tied down started to slowly come undone.

"What's going on in there Doctor?" General Mason asked as he oversaw from the glass he was behind passing back and forth.

Don looked at the computer to see how the virus he had made was working, then said in a panic, "It would seem, General, that the virus is starting to have a negative reaction in tandem with fighting off the disease."

The heart monitor started to beat more aggressively as it gradually got louder and louder then there was silence in the observation room.

"I need you to elaborate Dr. Rah. What do you mean?" General Mason questioned as his eyes were glued to what was going on in the room.

"Well, the virus started to take out the contagious disease but then something strange happened. There was another virus already within our subject that we did not account for. Even her heart has stopped. Things might still get a little chaotic," Don explained to the General as the eyes of the subject rolled in the back of her head and she broke free from her restraints.

The skin of the subject started to turn from a nice villain white to an appalling dark almost charcoal skin tone as she started running around the room and biting other researchers turning them into zombies faster than when the subject turned.

"You're fired Dr. Rah!" yelled General Mason.

Don had taken some of the serum that he had created and hid it in his pocket. After losing his job, Don had been re-creating a new serum to survive the X Serum and the vial he made was a light green.

"Let this one be uplifting and our saving grace." he had said, and he was going by a new name— a code name known as Wolfgang after Mozart.

DREAM OF DANGER

As I am jolted awake from a terrifying dream, drenched in a cold sweat in my room's cold darkness, I think back on the dream I had just woken up from. I felt the bumpiness of the black charcoal tires on the asphalt road, for I could not see anything in front of me due to a black mask that blocked my field of vision. I hear what seem to be people talking, but I could not tell. It sounded like their voices were muffled. Soon the vehicle came to a leeching stop as my body shifted forward and slammed hard against a leathery seat. The door swung open as cold air invaded the vehicle, nipping at my cheeks and fingers.

"Out of the car now," said a rough man's voice to me.

I slowly take one foot out of the vehicle. I hear a crunch under my foot. I think that might have been snow or even leaves from fall, something with cold fingers wrapped around my forearm tightly and yanked me out of the vehicle. I fell to my knees as I was yanked out and I thought to myself "Is this how I die not being able to see my killer's face? Well, at least my life was a happy and well-lived one."

"Help me get him up. Our boss wants him alive." A strong womanly voice said to the man.

"Ok, ok grab his left arm. I'll grab his right arm." The man instructed the woman.

When I was lifted from the ground, I found myself stumbling over large stones that were stairs. I hear the clanking of chains as a metal gate had opened and warm air surrounded me like a fresh blanket coming out of the drier blocking the cold air from getting to me. I was shoved inside, and I could hear the embers sizzling and bursting apart as the roar of new frames emerge. I continue to walk down a hallway and was stopped by a guarded woman on my left side. The punching of numbers on a keypad, then a door slide open, my hand had something round and hard. Something grabbed the top of my mask and yanked it hard off my head. I blinked my eyes to get a good fix of where I was, and I realize that I was standing in a big room with the lights turned off. The only light I could see was from the doors that I entered through. I turn to the shadows of a woman and a man looking back at me with their sparkling white teeth and both said in unison "Good luck on surviving."

"Survive what?" I shouted.

A booming voice came out of nowhere.

"You, sir, have to survive the boss level in this life-or -death game. All you and your team have to do is get to your friends in the panic box and you just have to avoid monsters and obstacles."

A blinding white light flashed on as I covered my eyes. When I was able to see again, I realized that I had an apple in my right hand as I bit into it. The sweet juice reminded me of an old apple-picking orchard. My team and I made it past the spinning death blades, ninja tennis fight, and rhythm wall. My team consisted of a tall muscular man with a shotgun, a little girl with long orange hair and in her hands was a massive double-edged sword, an athletic woman with short black hair holding two pistols, and me with a belt of grenades slung across my right shoulder down to my left hip.

We stood in front of an empty hallway and the muscular man on my team said, "What are we waiting for? Your friends are right in front of us. Let's get them." He took one step and dark monstrous creators started walking out of the walls glaring their red eyes at us. A woman with gray skin, long black hair, skinny legs, and six arms slowly rose from under the floor. All that stood between us and her were mirrors and ladders. When the rest of my team saw this woman, they dropped their weapons and ran back the way we came.

"Cowards!" I yelled to them.

The hallway had gone dark and all I saw were the woman's purple eyes and the shadow creators' red eyes. As I ran towards the woman, I slid on my knees under a ladder, pulled a grenade out of a pouch on the belt, yanked the pin, and threw the ticking bomb at the woman. She batted to grenade behind her making it land in an army of shadows, when the grenade went off, I ran right for the woman jumped straight over her and the smell of crushed peppers flew into my nose, and it burned like someone had poured hot sauce down my throat. The burning sensation was unbearable.

I reached the panic box and saw my friends Ka'shenia and Elizabeth reading magazines. I opened the door screaming "guys we have to get out of here." But it was like they did not even hear me. I repeated myself and Elizabeth said "We heard you, Wesley" as she stood up and walked toward me. A sharp pain shot through my body and when I looked down, I saw that I had been impaled and my legs started walking to Elizabeth. The upper half of my body started to crawl away from her. Elizabeth somehow got in front of me with a sword held high above her head then darkness. I sat straight up in my bed in sweat as I glanced at my alarm clock which read 4:25 am.